Little Red Riding Boots

by

Erin Zwiener

A Once Upon the West Fairy Tale

Illustrations by Merisha Sequoia Lemmer

THE ROADRUNNER PRESS
OKLAHOMA CITY, OKLAHOMA

Published by The RoadRunner Press

Catalog-in-Publication Data is on file at OCLC and SkyRiver and viewable at www.WorldCat.org

First Edition | Printed in November 2013 in the USA
by Bang Printing, Brainerd, Minnesota

ISBN: 978-1-937054-70-0 | LCCN: 2013950404

10 9 8 7 6 5 4 3 2 1

For Jaye.

You believed in this book

before I did.

Once there was a young cowgirl who lived on the range with her family.

She worked hard tending the ranch animals.

And everywhere she went she wore her bright red boots

with jangling silver spurs and a five-gallon hat.

(Ten-gallon hats being much too big for little girls.)

No chore, no matter how dirty, no matter how clean

could keep her out of those boots, so her family and friends

came to call her Little Red Riding Boots.

One day, Little Red Riding Boots decided to visit her pony, Fanny, who lived

in a nearby meadow. Fanny was a palomino with four white socks

and a mane and tail as fine as cream gravy.

Mother packed a knapsack full of carrots and apples for

Little Red Riding Boots to share with her pony and reminded her daughter,

"Keep your hat down to keep the sun off. Follow the creek path.

Don't dawdle along the way. And don't talk to strangers."

Little Red Riding Boots set off down the trail, lasso in hand.

As she walked, she spied a field of Indian Blanket blossoms.

The wildflowers would look fetching in Fanny's mane and tail, she thought.

Forgetting her mother's instructions, Little Red Riding Boots stopped to gather the flowers.

Nearby, a hungry mountain lion heard
the lilt of a little girl's voice singing an old cowboy song.

Careful not to startle the little girl,
the mountain lion said, with a false grin,
"Howdy! What brings you out on this fine day?"

Little Red Riding Boots was much too busy
smelling her flowers to remember her mother's
warning about not talking to strangers.
(She also wasn't certain furry strangers counted.)

"I'm on my way to visit my pony, Fanny," she said.
"She's the purtiest pony in all the West.
Don't you think these wildflowers will look
beautiful in her mane and tail?"

The mountain lion thought fast. If he played
his cards right, maybe he could have
the pony for lunch and the girl for supper, too.

"Oh yes," he said with a little smile. "You're one lucky
cowgirl to have the purtiest pony in all the West.
Where, may I ask, does the lovely Fanny live?"

Nose in her bouquet again,

Little Red Riding Boots missed the gleam in his eyes.

"In the meadow where the creek meets the river."

She glanced at the sun, now low in the sky.

"I'm late, and Fanny will be missing me," she said. "I better skedaddle."

And with a wave of her hat, she scampered off.

With his tummy growling, the mountain lion followed.

Only he took a shortcut across the range to Fanny's meadow.

There he crouched in the tall grass and edged

his way to where the pony grazed.

Using his best little girl voice, he called out,

"Ready to go for a ride, Fanny?"

Fanny turned expecting to see Little Red Riding Boots,

but instead of her sweet cowgirl, a mountain lion stood.

Before Fanny could even whinny, the mountain lion pounced and swallowed Fanny whole.

Smacking his lips, the mountain lion next laid his trap for Little Red Riding Boots . . .

He grabbed handfuls of tall grass and tucked them around his neck and into his tail.

He swung Fanny's saddle onto his back and slid her bridle over his ears.

He looked at his reflection in the nearby creek: A decent likeness for a pony, he thought.

Little Red Riding Boots skipped into view with a bunch of carrots for Fanny,

but not without noticing her pony looked a tad strange today.

Little Red Riding Boots stopped short and peered at the little

horse more closely — the better to see her.

"Howdy, Fanny," she called out.

"How's the grass today?"

"Just as grassy as always, darlin'," the mountion lion replied.

"Hurry over, so we can go for a ride!"

Little Red Riding Boots shook her head
as she eyed the creature before her.
"Oh, let me admire you for a few minutes more, Fanny.
What a lovely long tail you have."

"The better to swish the flies, darlin',"
the mountain lion replied.

"Oh, what fluffy, furry hooves you have,"
said Little Red Riding Boots.

"The better to stay warm in the winter,
darlin'," the lion said, edging closer.

"What big white teeth you have,"
Little Red Riding Boots observed.

"The better to eat you with, darlin'!"

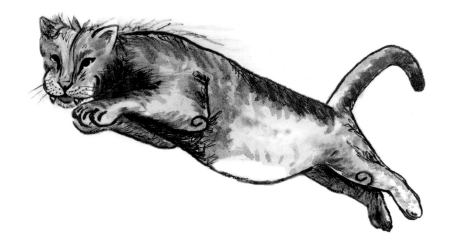

With that, the mountion lion shook off his disguise
and leapt high in the air, ready to pounce on Little Red Riding Boots.

But Little Red Riding Boots was on to the crafty mountain lion . . .
and while the mountain lion was still airbound,
she let her lasso fly, looping the lariat around his hind legs.

Quicker than a jackrabbit, Little Red Riding Boots
tossed the rope over the limb of a nearby tree and hauled the
mountain lion up until he was dangling a few feet off the ground.

"Did you eat my pony?" Little Red Riding Boots demanded.

"I might have," the lion snarled. "I was going to eat you, too, but I'm plum tuckered out from eating Fanny. She was quite the tasty snack."

Little Red Riding Boots said not a word but gave the mighty lion a no-you-didn't look. She grabbed her rope tighter and began to seesaw the lasso up and down, shaking the mountain lion to and fro.

All the motion made the mountain lion terribly sick to his tummy. Finally, the defeated lion cried, "You win!" He opened up his mouth and coughed Fanny out!

Little Red Riding Boots tied the rope off on a nearby tree,

leaving the mountain lion swinging in the air.

She gave Fanny a big hug and carefully checked her over.
Thankfully, her pony was unharmed.

Little Red Riding Boots squinted angrily at the mountain lion.
"Well now, what are we going to do with you?"

After conferring with Fanny, Little Red Riding Boots untied the rope from the tree

and gave it one good yank. The mountain lion came tumbling down.

Then she began twirling him over her head.

A cowpoke rounding up stray steers nearby had heard the ruckus and

wandered over to see what all the fuss was about. He poked his head

through the bushes just in time to see the mountain lion go flying

over the creek toward the next mountain range.

"Well, I guess it's not your first rodeo," he said, with a chuckle.

"Would you like an escort home, little lady?"

More mindful now of her mother's warning, Little Red Riding Boots shook her head.

"No, thank you, sir. I can see myself home."

The cowpoke tipped his hat and continued down the trail.
Fanny gave a little whinny and Little Red Riding Boots
gave her one last hug, before climbing onto
her beloved pony and heading west for home.

The bright red cowboy boots flashed against the pony's palomino coat

and the silver spurs jangled, as they road off into the sunset,

singing their favorite cowboy song.

Little Red Riding Boots

paid no mind to the airborne mountain lion

fading away in the distance.

The End